MW01232583

# Water Worlds
## Fresh Water

Peter Ampt

*for the Australian Museum*

This edition first published in 2002 in the United States of America by Chelsea House Publishers,
a subsidiary of Haights Cross Communications

Chelsea House Publishers
1974 Sproul Road, Suite 400
Broomall, PA 19008–0914

The Chelsea House world wide web address is www.chelseahouse.com

Library of Congress Cataloging-in-Publication Data Applied for.
ISBN 0-7910-6569-3


First published in 2000 by
Macmillan Education Australia Pty Ltd
627 Chapel Street, South Yarra, Australia, 3141

Copyright © Australian Museum 2000

Australian Museum Series Editor: Carolyn MacLulich
Australian Museum Scientific Adviser: Doug Hoese
Australian Museum Publishing Unit: Jenny Saunders and Kate Lowe

Edited by Anne McKenna
Typeset in Bembo
Printed in Hong Kong
Text and cover design by Leigh Ashforth @ watershed art & design
Illustrations by Peter Mather

## Acknowledgements

For Frances, Jeremy and Harriet, who love to explore rivers

The author would like to thank Martyn Robinson for his boundless knowledge
and willingness to share it, and Mandy Ampt for inspiration.

The author and publishers are grateful to the following for permission to use copyright material:
Front cover: .
      Main photo:      Jiri Lochman/Lochman Transparencies
      Inset photo:      Jean-Paul Ferrero/AUSCAPE
Back cover:      Roger Brown/AUSCAPE
Kathie Atkinson, pp. 5 (middle and bottom), 6, 11 (top and bottom), 12, 14, 17, 19 (bottom), 23 (bottom), 26
(bottom), 27, 28 (top and bottom); Kathie Atkinson/AUSCAPE, p. 9; Roger Brown/AUSCAPE, p. 7; Jean-Paul
Ferrero/AUSCAPE, pp. 15, 25; Francois Gohier/AUSCAPE, p. 8; Dennis Harding/AUSCAPE, p. 5 (top), 30; Wade
Hughes/Lochman Transparencies, p. 26 (top); Jean-Marc La Roque/AUSCAPE, p. 18; Wayne Lawler/AUSCAPE,
p. 10; Jiri Lochman/Lochman Transparencies, pp. 11 (middle), 13 (top), 19 (top), 20, 21, 22, 24 (left); Marie
Lochman/Lochman Transparencies, p. 23 (top); Dennis Sarson/Lochman Transparencies, pp. 3, 16, 24 (right),29;
Frank Woerle/AUSCAPE, p. 13 (bottom).

# Contents

# What are freshwater environments?

**Freshwater environments** are places where there is fresh water, with plants and animals living in and around the water. Fresh water contains little or no salts, so it would not taste salty if you drank it.

There are many different freshwater environments. Tiny mountain streams and mighty coastal rivers, waterfalls and stillwater ponds, lakes and underground rivers are just a few of the places through which fresh water flows on its long journey from the mountains to the sea.

Living things live and thrive around fresh water. The water helps plants grow and the plants provide food for animals. Animals also provide food for other animals.

≋ This diagram of the water cycle shows how water moves around the environment.

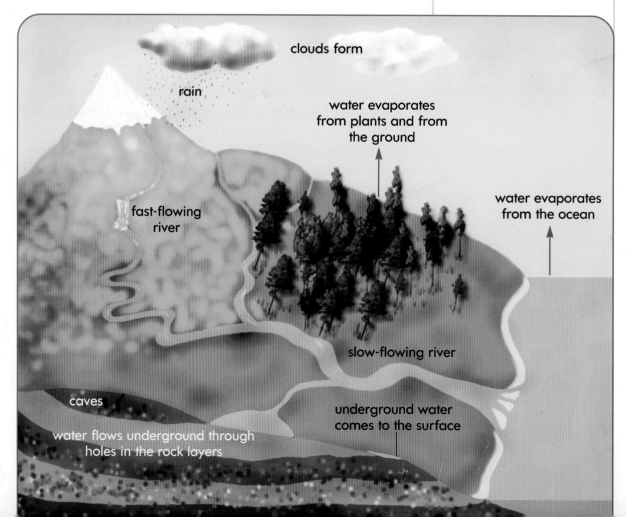

clouds form

rain

water evaporates from plants and from the ground

water evaporates from the ocean

fast-flowing river

slow-flowing river

caves

underground water comes to the surface

water flows underground through holes in the rock layers

≋ Many rivers start high in the mountains, where they are often fed by melting snow.

≋ As rivers flow through mountainous places, they often tumble over cliffs and form waterfalls like this one.

≋ As a river reaches flat country at the base of the mountains, it slows down, forming bends called **meanders**.

## Did you know?

*When it rains, much of the water that falls soaks into the ground. As the water flows through the ground, it **dissolves** salts from the ground and carries them to creeks and rivers. Eventually, the water and salt flow into the ocean. Over millions of years, these salts have built up in the ocean, making the water salty.*

# Mountain water

Mountain water is clear, clean and cold. Water from mist, rainwater and melting snow flows downhill until it gathers into small streams. Many living things that are adapted to the cold, including Corroboree Frogs, crayfish and trout, live in and around mountain streams.

## Did you know?

Cold water holds much more oxygen than warm water. All animals need oxygen, especially when they are young. As a result, cold mountain streams are excellent places for some animals to breed.

≋ This Corroboree Frog is in its nest with some of its eggs. The frog's bright colors are a warning not to eat the frog—it will taste awful and may even be poisonous.

The nest is in sphagnum (say: sfag-num) moss. This moss soaks up water like a giant sponge. It protects the fragile mountain soils from wind and rain. Many other animals, such as ants and snails, also live in this moss.

≋ Many freshwater crayfish live in mountain streams where they thrive in the cold, fast-flowing water. They build burrows in the banks that are so narrow they have to do somersaults to turn around!

## Life cycle of a trout

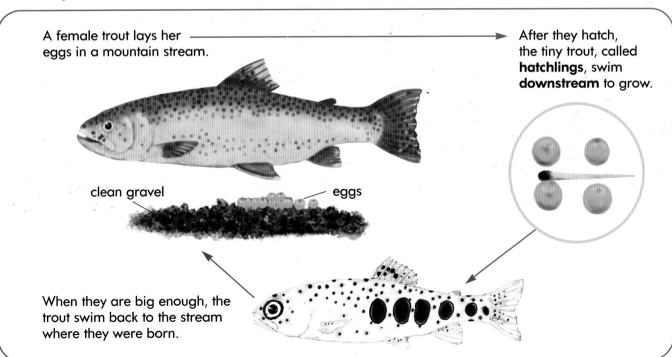

A female trout lays her eggs in a mountain stream.

After they hatch, the tiny trout, called **hatchlings**, swim **downstream** to grow.

clean gravel        eggs

When they are big enough, the trout swim back to the stream where they were born.

# Fast-flowing rivers

As water flows from the mountains to the sea, it often tumbles down narrow valleys in fast-flowing rivers and streams. Animals and plants that live in these streams have adapted to the strong current so they do not get washed away. Some fish, such as salmon and trout, can even swim fast enough to go **upstream** through small waterfalls!

≋ Salmon and trout move fast enough to leap over and swim through small waterfalls. These Sock-eye Salmon have swum up the river from the ocean. They swim upstream to mate and lay their eggs in a mountain stream. They can travel thousands of kilometres in their lifetime.

Animals that do not move around as adults have evolved some interesting ways to mate in fast-flowing water. Freshwater mussels make lots of sperm that they squirt into the water. As the sperm floats in the water, it may be sucked in by other mussels to fertilize the eggs inside them.

## Life cycle of a freshwater mussel

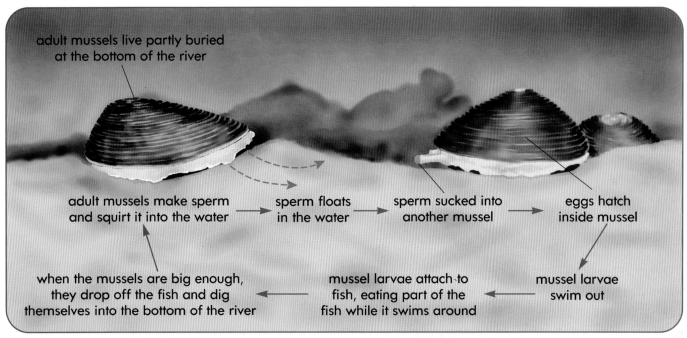

adult mussels live partly buried at the bottom of the river

adult mussels make sperm and squirt it into the water → sperm floats in the water → sperm sucked into another mussel → eggs hatch inside mussel

when the mussels are big enough, they drop off the fish and dig themselves into the bottom of the river ← mussel larvae attach to fish, eating part of the fish while it swims around ← mussel larvae swim out

≋ Freshwater mussels live in fast-flowing rivers by burying themselves in the bottom and clinging on with their **muscular** foot. They get food by sucking water in through a tube and filtering out tiny particles of food to eat. They spit the water out through another tube.

# Slow-flowing rivers

As a river reaches the flat land at the base of the mountains it slows down. The long, slow-moving stretches of water are usually surrounded by large trees and abundant life.

Sometimes, very large fish live in slow-flowing rivers. For example, Murray Cod are one of the biggest freshwater fish in the world. They live in the Murray-Darling river system in eastern Australia. Murray Cod can grow to a massive 90 kilograms (200 pounds) in large rivers. A female can produce up to 200,000 eggs at mating time.

≋ These tall forests of Red Gum trees live around a slow-flowing river.

≋ Water Monitors spend most of their time in rivers and billabongs. Like crocodiles, their eyes and nose are in line so they can swim with them both just above water. This makes it easier to sneak up on their food.

≋ Many animals wait on the edges of rivers for food to pass by. Water Dragons eat flying and swimming insects that live in and around the river water.

## Environment alert!

*Sometimes blue-green **algae** (say: al-gee) grow very rapidly in rivers. This can occur in rivers that slow down, warm up and contain lots of phosphate (say: fos-fait) and other **nutrients**. The algae produce a **toxin** that can kill animals, including people, who drink the water.*

*People contribute or even cause the problem of algae by:*
* *using detergents that contain phosphates;*
* *using too much phosphate **fertilizer** on their farms;*
* *slowing down rivers by building dams and using river water for irrigating farms.*

# Billabongs

**Billabongs** are small lakes that form when slow-flowing rivers change course and sections get cut off from the rest of the river. Billabongs are often surrounded by lots of trees. They attract plenty of wildlife, such as birds and snakes. This wildlife comes to eat the millions of insects and other animals that thrive in and around the water of the billabong.

≋ Birds flock to billabongs. These Little Corellas are small parrots that live in flocks of up to 20,000 birds.

Even in very dry places, lots of plants grow in and around billabongs.

Water Pythons live around billabongs waiting for food to pass by. This Water Python has just swallowed a duck. Snakes swallow their food whole, and when the meat is digested, they get rid of the bones and feathers in their feces.

# Animals that walk on water

In the still waters of ponds and billabongs, there are many animals that can walk on water! By walking on water they can catch and eat animals that fly down to the water surface or swim up to the surface from under water.

Water surfaces have an invisible 'skin' caused by **surface tension**. Water striders and water spiders can walk on top of the invisible 'skin' because they are very light and they have millions of tiny hairs on their long legs which **repel** water.

≋ Water striders skate across the surface of the water to catch small insects.

14

## Environment alert!

*Cleaning products break up the surface tension of water. Also, oil floats on the surface of water, making it unsuitable for most water life.*

*To help protect water life, you should never pour oil down the drain. Also, if you use **biodegradable** detergents they will break down quickly before they harm water life.*

≋ This water spider has caught a small fish. It waited on the water surface, with its front legs ready to grab the fish when it came close enough.

# Wetlands

**Wetlands** are areas of land, such as swamps and marshes, that remain wet and muddy all year round.

Wetlands are an essential environment for hundreds of different living things. This is because they have permanent water, abundant nutrients and plentiful food available all year round. Many birds, for example, would not survive without wetlands. Some **migrating** birds even travel thousands of miles back to the same wetland every year to feed and mate.

≋ There are many types of animals on this wetland in Kakadu National Park, Australia.

Wetlands and the trees that surround them help keep rivers healthy. They filter out polluting chemicals and help reduce flooding. In dry times, water continues to drain slowly out of them. This helps maintain the water level in rivers and also helps supply underground water.

≋ This snake is hunting in a swamp for birds, small fish, lizards or frogs.

## Environment alert!

Many wetlands have been destroyed or **degraded** by people:
• building new developments such as housing estates on them;
• changing the flow of rivers that supply them with water;
• clearing trees that surround them.

# Coping with floods

Floods can be major disasters for people. They can destroy houses, damage roads and kill livestock. But for **native** plants and animals, floods are part of the environment they live in, and they have many ways of coping with floods. In fact, many rely on floods for their survival.

Lungfish live in coastal rivers and streams. They often become stranded in ponds and billabongs that are drying up. They have **lungs** as well as **gills**, so they can gulp air to survive as their waterhole dries up. Eventually, they need a flood to rescue them so they can return to the river. For a stranded lungfish, floods are a lifesaver!

≋ These cattle have become stranded by rising floodwaters.

≋ This Black-headed Python is clinging to a branch so that it is not washed away by the flood.

≋ Lungfish are often rescued from dry waterholes by floodwaters.

## Environment alert!

People try to prevent floods because floods can cause death and destruction. For example, they build dams across rivers so that they can catch extra water and stop it from causing floods.

However, for many freshwater environments, floods are an essential part of the natural cycle. Preventing floods can harm these environments.

# When ponds dry up

In times when there has been a lot of rain, there is plenty of
food for animals to eat and ponds are often full of life. But
there are times when the weather stays hot and the land
starts to dry up. Sometimes a pond might only last for a few
weeks, then dry up for months or even years. Grass stops
growing and turns brown. When this happens, most of the
animals disappear. Then when it rains, within a short time,
the land is teeming with life again. Where did all that life
come from, and where does it go when it is dry?

≋ These kangaroos are drinking from a puddle in a drying creek bed.
In dry times when food is scarce, kangaroo babies stop growing inside
their mothers. Then, when rains come and food is plentiful, the baby
will start to grow again and be born. In this way, the kangaroo
**population** can increase quickly when there is enough food.

≋ These Shield Shrimps are living in a pond that is about to dry up. Very soon they will all be dead. The pond may remain dry for years but when it does rain, thousands of baby Shield Shrimps will reappear in the pond.

## Life cycle of Shield Shrimps

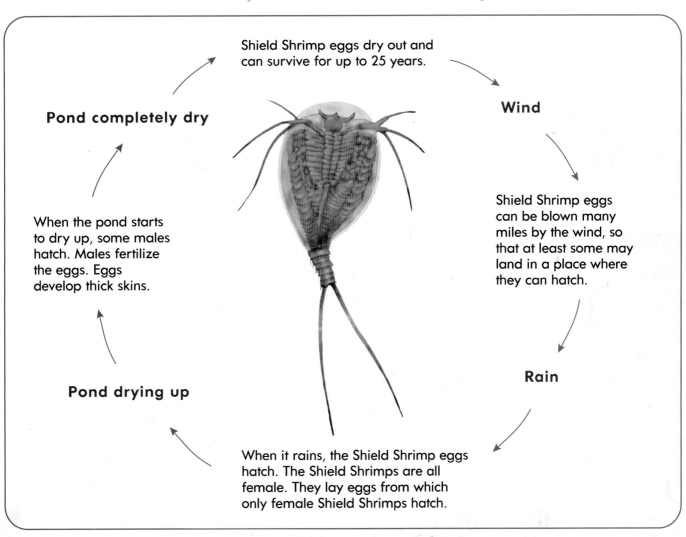

Shield Shrimp eggs dry out and can survive for up to 25 years.

**Pond completely dry**

When the pond starts to dry up, some males hatch. Males fertilize the eggs. Eggs develop thick skins.

**Pond drying up**

**Wind**

Shield Shrimp eggs can be blown many miles by the wind, so that at least some may land in a place where they can hatch.

**Rain**

When it rains, the Shield Shrimp eggs hatch. The Shield Shrimps are all female. They lay eggs from which only female Shield Shrimps hatch.

# Freshwater life in the desert

Deserts are places where rain hardly ever falls. Sometimes it does not rain at all for several years. The plants that survive in deserts are small and hardy, with roots that grow deep down into the ground to where there is just enough water for them to live.

However, when it rains in the desert, wildflowers appear everywhere within days and ponds are soon full of animal life. These living things have to grow and mate quickly, because the water in the ponds and the ground will soon dry up.

Burrowing frogs, for example, survive dry times by filling themselves full of water and burrowing into the mud as their pond dries up. If they are big enough, they survive underground until the next rain.

≋ Lakes in the desert usually remain dry for most of the year.

LAKE DISAPPOINTMENT

≋ When it rains in the desert, it often floods. The animals and plants come quickly to life and birds fly in from miles away to feed.

## Life cycle of a burrowing frog

frogs come out from underground and females lay eggs

males fertilize the eggs

**Rain**

tadpoles hatch from the eggs

frogs stay buried for many months or years

tadpoles grow quickly and change into frogs

**Pond completely dry**

frogs grow quickly

frogs burrow deep in the mud

**Pond drying up**

# Underground water

When rain falls on the ground, some of the water soaks into the ground and flows underground. It flows through rock with lots of holes, cracks and caves in it. This underground water can flow for many thousands of miles. Sometimes it comes to the surface as **springs**. In other places, it forms huge underground lakes. The top level of this underground water is called the **water table**. Despite being underground, there are still animals that live in this water.

Removing trees can cause the underground water to rise. This can lead to salt crusts on the surface of the soil. This is called dryland **salinity** and the salt can kill trees and prevent other plants from growing. If dryland salinity occurs, people need to plant many trees in the right place to reduce the amount of water entering the underground rivers. To prevent dryland salinity, people need to stop removing trees.

≋ People use windmills to pump underground water to the surface. The water from underground is called bore water.

≋ Sometimes when underground water reaches the surface, it is hot. Even in this hot water, some creatures can live.

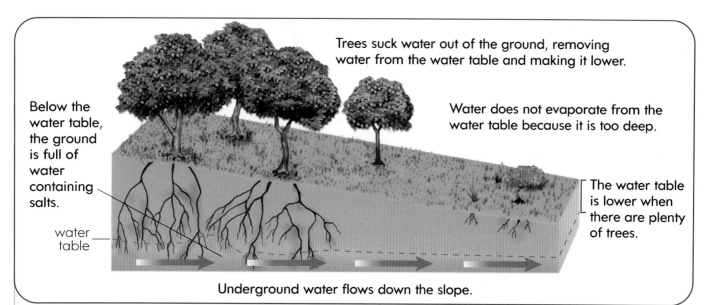

Trees suck water out of the ground, removing water from the water table and making it lower.

Below the water table, the ground is full of water containing salts.

Water does not evaporate from the water table because it is too deep.

water table

The water table is lower when there are plenty of trees.

Underground water flows down the slope.

≋ This diagram shows how trees help to keep the water table well below the surface of the ground.

≋ This diagram shows how the removal of trees causes the water table to rise.

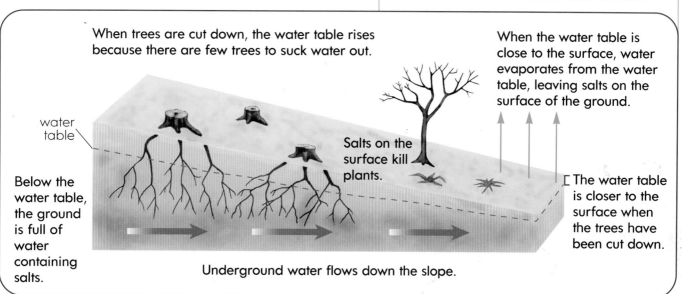

When trees are cut down, the water table rises because there are few trees to suck water out.

When the water table is close to the surface, water evaporates from the water table, leaving salts on the surface of the ground.

water table

Salts on the surface kill plants.

Below the water table, the ground is full of water containing salts.

The water table is closer to the surface when the trees have been cut down.

Underground water flows down the slope.

≋ For thousands of years, salty underground water has been coming to the surface in this desert. The mound has been formed from salt deposited around the spring. Algae, tiny shrimps and fish called gobies live in mound springs. Water plants, such as reeds, live in and around mound springs.

# Freshwater life in the city

In cities, people change freshwater environments. We:

- build walls on the river banks to stop rivers from changing direction;
- turn creeks into stormwater drains;
- drain wetlands, and fill in the land to build houses, shops and factories;
- drop litter on the ground and it gets washed into creeks, rivers and ponds;
- put detergents and other chemicals down our drains and they **pollute** our waterways.

All of these actions destroy or degrade places for animals and plants to live.

≋ Water beetles thrive in ponds, eating the green, slimy algae that cling to rocks in the water. They, in turn, attract other insects, tadpoles and small fish that feed on them.

≋ Freshwater worms live in small ponds. They feed on tiny bits of dead plants and animals in the mud on the bottom of the pond. Worms get eaten by insects and small fish.

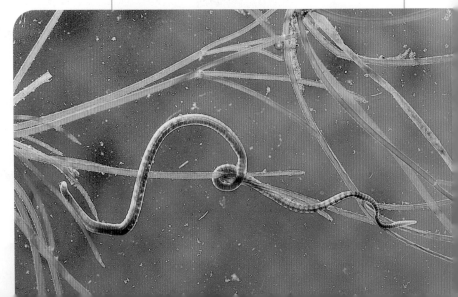

## A backyard pond

But even a small pond in a backyard can make a difference. If you put water plants, snails and a few fish in the pond, before long you will find lots of other animals in it as well. Birds, frogs and many insects will visit your pond and many will stay and make it their home.

≋ Small garden ponds can increase the wildlife in your garden and in your neighborhood.

## Life in a pond

≋ You might find any of these living things in a small pond.

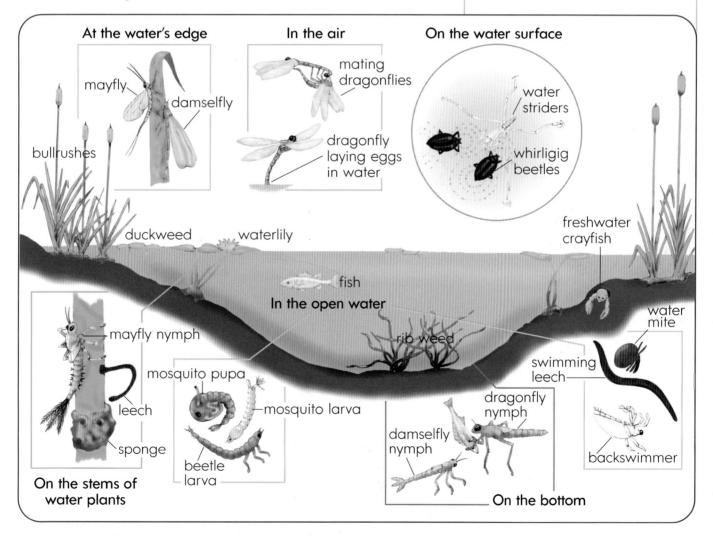

**At the water's edge**

mayfly

damselfly

bullrushes

**In the air**

mating dragonflies

dragonfly laying eggs in water

**On the water surface**

water striders

whirligig beetles

duckweed    waterlily

freshwater crayfish

fish

**In the open water**

water mite

rib weed

mayfly nymph

mosquito pupa

leech

sponge

mosquito larva

beetle larva

**On the stems of water plants**

swimming leech

dragonfly nymph

damselfly nymph

backswimmer

**On the bottom**

# Fresh water for people

People living in cities and towns need water for drinking, washing, flushing the toilet and gardening. Farmers need water for their animals to drink and may use water to **irrigate** their crops so that they will grow better.

To supply this water, people make lakes by building big dams across rivers, then build pipes or **canals** to carry the water to where it is needed. The water that comes out of your tap has probably travelled all the way from a lake to your home through pipes.

≋ In many parts of Australia, crops are grown in places that used to be like deserts. Irrigation has turned this land near Bourke in inland New South Wales into productive farmland.

≋ Poor management of water can cause land to be degraded by salt. In this photo the plants are dying because salt is collecting on the surface of the land. This has occurred because too much water has caused the water table to rise, bringing salt with it.

🌊 Building dams can create huge lakes, such as Lake Argyle in Western Australia.

## Environment alert!

Damming rivers can cause the river to start to dry up further **downstream**.

Irrigating from the same river many times causes the river water to get saltier. This is because the water will flow through the soil back to the river many times, dissolving a little more salt each time. By the time the river reaches the ocean, it can be too salty for irrigation or drinking.

# Environment watch

## Why are freshwater environments important?

Freshwater environments provide places for many plants and animals to live. Many other animals, such as migrating birds, visit them to feed or rest. If we do not conserve freshwater environments, many of these plants and animals will become endangered or may even die out altogether.

If we keep freshwater environments healthy, we can make sure that we have a supply of clean, fresh water for ourselves as well. We can also enjoy the beauty of freshwater environments with their fascinating variety of life.

## Things You Can Do
### to help protect freshwater environments

**Households can:**
- ◇ Use low-phosphate cleaning products that are biodegradable.
- ◇ Not use too much detergent.
- ◇ Not put oil down the drain.
- ◇ Have a pond in the garden.

**Farmers and other landholders can:**
- ◇ Avoid removing trees.
- ◇ Plant more trees in the right places.
- ◇ Use irrigation water carefully.
- ◇ Use phosphate fertilizers carefully.

**Environmental planners and politicians can:**
- ◇ Keep rivers flowing.
- ◇ Allow rivers to flood.
- ◇ Protect wetlands.

# Glossary

| | |
|---|---|
| **algae** | plants, such as seaweeds, that live in wet conditions and do not have leaves, stems or roots |
| **billabongs** | small lakes or ponds |
| **biodegradable** | materials that break down quickly in the environment |
| **canals** | channels that people have made to carry water from one place to another |
| **degraded** | when something is damaged so that it cannot function properly any more |
| **dissolves** | mixes with water and disappears |
| **downstream** | further down a river |
| **fertilizer** | chemicals that people spread on the ground to help plants grow |
| **freshwater environments** | places where there is fresh water, with plants and animals living in and around the water |
| **gills** | parts of an animal that help it breathe in water |
| **hatchlings** | young fish that have just hatched from eggs |
| **irrigate** | put water on the ground to help plants grow |
| **lungs** | parts of an animal that help it breathe in air |
| **meanders** | big bends in a river |
| **migrating** | moving long distances from one place to another |
| **muscular** | with muscles |
| **native** | a living thing that belongs to a particular place |
| **nutrients** | chemicals in the environment that living things need to grow |
| **pollute** | to put things in the environment that are harmful to it |
| **population** | a group of living things in a particular place |
| **repel** | push away |
| **salinity** | the amount of salt that is in water |
| **springs** | places where water from under the ground flows onto the surface of the ground |
| **surface tension** | a type of force-field, made by water molecules tending to stick together, which forms an invisible 'skin' on the water |
| **toxin** | a chemical that can harm living things |
| **upstream** | further up a river |
| **water table** | a level under the ground, below which the ground is saturated with water |
| **wetlands** | places that are always wet, for example, swamps and marshes |

# Index